At last, Eddie and Marie were able to see where the voices were coming from. Norton and Marigold Bicker were standing near the trash can, and they were eight inches tall. Marigold was an eight-inch woman in a checkered dress and tiny fluffy bedroom slippers. Norton was an eight-inch man with a bald head and tiny glasses.

"Uh-oh," said Marie. "We've got trouble now."

And her parents were still shrinking . . .

THE
TINY
PARENTS

ELLEN WEISS & MEL FRIEDMAN

BULLSEYE BOOKS · ALFRED A. KNOPF
New York

DR. M. JERRY WEISS, Distinguished Service Professor of Communications at Jersey City State College, is the educational consultant for Bullseye Books. Currently chair of the International Reading Association President's Advisory Committee on Intellectual Freedom, he travels frequently to give workshops on the use of trade books in schools.

A BULLSEYE BOOK PUBLISHED BY ALFRED A. KNOPF, INC.
Text copyright © 1989 by Ellen Weiss and Mel Friedman
Cover art copyright © 1989 by Mark Buehner

Library of Congress Cataloging-in-Publication Data
Weiss, Ellen. The tiny parents. (Bullseye books) Summary: When, after an experiment goes wrong, their inventor parents shrink until they are only two and a half inches tall, it's up to twelve-year-old Marie and nine-year-old Eddie to figure out how to get them back to normal. [1. Inventors—Fiction. 2. Size—Fiction. 3. Parent and child—Fiction. 4. Humorous stories] I. Friedman, Mel. II. Title. PZ7.W4472Ti 1989 [Fic] 88-23103 ISBN 0-394-82418-0 (pbk.) ISBN 0-394-92418-5 (lib. bdg.)

RL: 4.9

Manufactured in the United States of America
0   1   2   3   4   5   6   7   8   9

❧ *To Nora and Nadja* ❧

Contents

THE
TINY
PARENTS

CHAPTER ONE

The Weirdest Parents in New York

The Bickers were at it again.

"Norton Bicker, I just don't know what you use for brains sometimes! The epsilon confabulator goes on the other end!"

"You don't know what you're talking about, Marigold—as usual! Do you want to blow us up? The epsilon confabulator goes on *this* end. And *you* pointed the vector field in the wrong direction!"

"I did not!"

"Did too!"

"Did not!"

"Did too!"

"Did not did not did not!"

Upstairs, on the second floor of the tall, narrow brownstone house in Brooklyn, Eddie and Marie Bicker were trying to do their homework.

"I've had it," said Marie, throwing down her pencil. "How can I think about the Mexican Revolution when they're screaming downstairs in the basement? You know what I'm going to do? I'm going to walk down the block and look in windows, and when I find a really normal-looking family, eating Pop-Tarts and feeding their goldfish, I'm going to knock on their door and ask if I can live with them."

The night outside was dark and bitter cold. Marie looked at her reflection in the frost-covered window, and a perfectly normal-looking twelve-year-old girl looked back at her. Well, of course her nose *was* just a little too large. She rolled her eyes.

"All I want is to have normal parents, like other kids. Is that too much to ask?"

"Umm," said Eddie, chewing his pencil absently. Basil, their aging basset hound, lay at his feet chewing on Eddie's slipper.

Marie knew there was no point in continuing the discussion. Being normal was not something that particularly interested Eddie. He wasn't stupid—in fact, he was probably the smartest kid in the fourth grade at P. S. 217—but he just didn't care about the finer things in life. He could wear the same mismatched pair of socks for two weeks and not notice. And it didn't much bother him that he probably had the weirdest parents in New York City.

A crash sounded from downstairs.

"You potato-head!"

"You slug!"

"You—you wing nut!"

Eddie twirled one of his curls around his finger and didn't look up from his reading. "You know they don't really mean it," he said. "Besides, they'd never get anything invented if they didn't scream at each other." He breathed on his glasses and rubbed them with his shirttail, which just made them smearier.

"Would that be so terrible?" demanded Marie. "I don't know about you, but *I* think the world could survive without an electronic toothpaste-tube roller or a mechanical pillow fluffer."

"This one's really important to them,

though," said Eddie. "This one would change the world. They'd be famous."

"You want to know what I think? I think it's scary, that's what I think."

"It does have a bit of risk attached to it, I guess."

"A bit of risk," snorted Marie. "A bit of risk. Remember what happened when they tested the first model? On the cheeseburger? It took us three days to clean it up. And remember trying to get rid of all those six-pound sesame seeds without attracting the neighbors' attention?"

"Well, they did say it needed a little adjustment."

"I hope the Proton Enlarger never gets built. Some scientific advances should never be unleashed on the world. Especially a machine with a ray that makes things bigger."

There was a loud bang from the basement, and then an earsplitting electronic hum. "Not that switch, the other one!" yelled Marigold.

"What? I can't hear you!" shouted Norton.

"Pull it, you dim-bulb! Pull it now!"

"What? What?"

"Quick, before it's too late! The ray! Oh, nooo!"

Eddie sat up in his seat, finally paying attention. "Does something sound funny about their voices?" he asked Marie.

"Wait a second, let me listen," she whispered.

There was silence for a moment.

"Now look what you've done!" shrieked Marigold.

Eddie blinked. "Don't their voices sound sort of . . . high?"

"Yeah. Kind of . . . tiny," agreed Marie. They looked at each other.

Then they sprang out of their chairs and barreled downstairs, tripping all over Basil in their rush to get to the basement. When they got to the heavily padded door at the bottom of the stairs, they burst into the laboratory. The lab was even messier than usual: there were test tubes, beakers, flywheels, gears, bent spoons, and plungers everywhere.

But Norton and Marigold weren't there.

"Good lord," whispered Marie. "They've vaporized themselves."

They stood there silently, in awe and terror.

"We haven't vaporized ourselves," said a small, squeaky voice from somewhere near the trash can. "Your *father* attached the 'on' switch upside down."

"That's because your *mother* bought the wrong kind of switch at the hardware store," said another voice in tiny fury.

"That's because your *father* wrote down the wrong thing on the shopping list," said the first little voice.

"That's because your *mother* was rushing me, as usual," said the second voice.

At last, Eddie and Marie were able to see where the voices were coming from. Norton and Marigold Bicker were standing near the trash can, and they were eight inches tall. Marigold was an eight-inch woman in a checkered dress and tiny fluffy bedroom slippers. Norton was an eight-inch man with a bald head and tiny glasses.

"Uh-oh," said Marie. "We've got trouble now."

"It's not my fault," squeaked Marigold.

"Well, then, whose fault is it, Mrs. Brilliant Inventor?" squeaked Norton.

They went on like this for a minute, screaming and jumping up and down, until Eddie broke in.

"HOLD IT!" he yelled. "JUST SHUT UP FOR A SECOND, WILL YOU?"

They shut up, surprised.

"Look at yourselves," he said. "You're still shrinking! You were as tall as that pile of newspapers a minute ago, and now you only come halfway up it! You're getting shorter every second. We'll have to do something fast, or you really will disappear."

"Oh God," said Norton. "Oh God, oh God."

"Quick," ordered Marigold. "Run over and reverse the field alternator, Eddie! The red button."

Eddie leaped to the machine and punched the large red button. There was a small popping noise, but nothing happened.

"Try the polar multiplexer," suggested Norton. "The big black switch with the bobby pin sticking out."

Eddie pushed the switch up. There were a lot of sparks, and then all the lights went off on the machine.

"We're still shrinking," squeaked Marigold, an edge of hysteria creeping into her voice. "We're only three newspapers high now!"

"Time for desperate measures," said Marie. "Try kicking it."

Eddie shrugged. "Nothing to lose," he said, and gave the machine a tremendous kick that made him dance with pain. This time the machine hiccuped. "Ow, ow, ow," moaned Eddie.

"You've done it," said Norton. "We've stopped shrinking!"

And a good thing, too. Norton and Marigold Bicker were now two and a half inches tall.

CHAPTER TWO

Hungry, Hungry, Hungry

There didn't seem to be much to say for a while. There was, however, a lot to think.

Eddie was thinking, Well, I'm nine years old, and Marie's twelve. I guess we can take care of ourselves. But how are we going to get the money to buy groceries? And what are we going to feed Norton and Marigold, anyway?

Marie was thinking, This would be a really good time to go find that nice, normal family. Yes, maybe this is really the day to do it.

It's impossible to say what Norton and Marigold were thinking.

"I have an idea," volunteered Eddie at last. "Maybe we could reverse the effects of the machine—make it do what it was supposed to do before it zapped you."

"You could try it," said Marigold. "Try flipping that red switch a couple of times."

Eddie flipped the switch. The machine didn't even blink.

"It's no good," said Norton mournfully. "The circuits are all fused now. The machine is gone. Dead. Defunct."

Marie sat down on a lab stool and stared into space. She tried to make sense of this new situation. My parents are two and a half inches tall, she imagined herself explaining to the people from the newspapers. Then she imagined making her little speech in a more casual tone of voice: Hi, I'm Marie Curie Bicker. My brother's name is Edison Newton Bicker. We're named for famous scientists, isn't that cute? Our parents are two and a half inches tall. She kept on staring into space, but her chin was trembling a little. The world was swimming in front of her eyes. "Yikes," she sighed. "This is bad."

"There, there, dear," said Marigold, in a rare moment of motherly tenderness. "It'll be all right. We'll figure something out. Here, pick me up."

Marie picked her up. "It's very high up here," squeaked Marigold, looking down.

Marie brought her mother very close to her face, and Marigold leaned over and kissed her on the cheek. "There, there, dear," she repeated.

"Ahem," said Norton. "Sorry to bring this up, but I'm awfully hungry."

"How can you think of food at a time like this?" asked Marigold.

"Well, I'm sorry, but I am. I really am," repeated Norton.

Marie stared into space, sniffing quietly. There was a long silence.

"You know something?" said Marigold. "I'm hungry too. I'm very, very hungry."

"It makes sense," reasoned Eddie, who had been thinking about it. "The tinier you are, the faster you burn up food. Little birds and mice and shrews and things, they have to eat practically all the time, just to keep their little hearts beating. All they do all day is look for bugs and stuff."

"Bugs? Yucch!" cried Marie, suddenly coming to life. "Eddie, we're not going to have to feed them *bugs*, are we?"

"I don't think so," said Eddie.

"We're still *people*, for heaven's sake," said Norton. "We'll need to eat people food. I wouldn't mind a nice bacon, lettuce, and tomato sandwich right now, to tell you the truth."

"I think a BLT might be a little hard for you to manage, Dad," said Marie. "Eddie and I better go upstairs and figure out something you *can* eat."

They started with the refrigerator. There were a lot of furry things in there. Norton and Marigold were not into housework.

"Old roast beef," said Eddie. "No good—we won't be able to cut it up small enough."

"What if they waste away in a couple of days?" said Marie.

"How about this cottage cheese?"

"What if they stay tiny forever?" said Marie.

"Don't think about it," said Eddie.

"Maybe the cottage cheese will work for Marigold," said Marie. "Norton hates cottage cheese. Why don't you give him some of that creamed spinach?"

"Each one of those little flakes of spinach is almost as big as his head," observed Eddie.

"Here, let's put all this stuff into the blender. That will smooth it out, and it'll be sort of balanced. Throw in this leftover oatmeal too. And those sardines, way in the back."

"This is going to get to be a big pain in the neck, very fast," said Eddie, dropping a teaspoonful of each thing into the blender. As a final touch, he shook in a few globs of ketchup. "There," he said, turning on the blender. "Now it has another vegetable."

Marie tasted it. "It's disgusting," she said. "Maybe some salt would help."

"We're out of salt," said Eddie. "I'll put in some pepper instead. It's the best we can do. They'll just have to eat whatever we can figure out."

"I have an idea," said Marie. "I'll run out to the store and buy a few jars of baby food. It's got to be better than this."

Marie put on her jacket, rummaged in the old glass beaker they used for spare money, and ran out the door. Eddie sat at the table for a while, scratching Basil behind his big, floppy ears and thinking about life. Idly, he stuck a finger into the foul-smelling glop. Could be worse, he thought. He rolled it around in his mouth and made a face. "Nope, couldn't be worse."

What would Julia Child do to give this dish a little extra something? he wondered. He opened the cupboard and took out a jar of strawberry jam. Perhaps just a suspicion of strawberry, he thought, stirring in a spoonful. And a dash of coconut for garnish. He sprinkled on a huge amount of the white flaky stuff.

Then he looked around the kitchen for something his parents could use for silverware and plates. His eye fell on a root-beer bottle cap that had been left lying on the counter. Okay, he thought, here's their plate. They can share it. Now what are they going to eat with?

After another few minutes of looking around, he had just about decided they'd have to eat with their fingers when he noticed a box of flat toothpicks on the shelf above the stove. He climbed up on a stool to get them. The box had sticky brown kitchen dirt all over it. He took out two toothpicks and broke off about a quarter of an inch from the end of each one. He filled the bottle cap with the greenish mush and stood the two toothpick pieces up in it, as attractively as he could. "*Bon appétit*," he muttered, and headed for the basement.

Downstairs, Norton and Marigold were

waiting impatiently for their dinner. They sat down on the floor, and Eddie placed the bottle cap between them.

"Boy oh boy, I can't believe how hungry I am," said Norton, shoveling the food into his mouth at an incredible rate.

"Me, too," agreed Marigold, eating just as quickly. "This stuff is horrible, Edison. Is there any more?"

"There's more in the blender," said Eddie. He was amazed at how much they'd eaten in thirty seconds. "I'll go get it."

He trudged upstairs, already feeling like a prisoner in a forced-labor camp. He could imagine himself spending his days and nights going up and down, up and down, the little voices chirping like baby birds for more and more and more. . . .

Marie came in and slammed the kitchen door, bringing in a cloud of cold air with her. Her hands were red when she pulled off her woolen gloves.

"I got Peas and Carrots, Squash, and look at this—Veal Dinner. Pretty good, huh?"

"Looks delicious," chuckled Eddie. "Especially those Peas and Carrots. Mmm-*mmmm*." If there was one good thing about this situation, it was the delightful feeling of revenge he was experiencing. He thought of all the times Norton had cooked liver and onions with wheat germ on top, and Marigold had made him eat it. Biologically correct food, they called it.

Marie sat down at the table. Eddie saw that she had an armful of bottles and jars, gathered from the forbidden top shelf of the cupboard. These were all the strange and mysterious foods Norton and Marigold kept for "special occasions"—red syrup to put into liquor, tiny onions, maraschino cherries, little silver balls for decorating cakes, and chocolate-covered after-dinner mints. She lined them all up in front of her on the table and stared hard at them for a few moments. Then she shrugged. "What the heck," she said, opening them up one by one. "Here goes nothing."

"Can I try one of those cherries?" asked Eddie.

"Sure," said Marie, digging into the mints.

"I wonder if those silver things are really edible," said Eddie, reaching for one. It was an incredible feeling, knowing that there was absolutely nobody to yell at them.

18

"You'll never guess what Mildred Grackle is doing now," Marie said conversationally, chewing noisily on a silver ball. Mildred Grackle lived in the house next door.

"I can hardly wait to find out. Is she raising catfish in her bathtub again?"

"No, this is even better. She's starting a lemming farm in her backyard."

"A lemming farm? What for?"

"She read someplace that lemmings have good fur for coats and they taste just like chicken. So she got five hundred of them from a mail-order catalog. The new guy that works in the store told me." She took a long swig of red syrup.

"Hold on. You mean lemmings, those little brown furry animals that jump into the ocean every few years? Those lemmings?"

"Those lemmings."

"Sheesh."

"Then again, who are we to call anyone else weird? Our parents are two and a half inches tall."

"Oh, nuts!" cried Eddie, jumping up from his chair. "I forgot about their next capful of food. They must be starving down there."

"I hope they like the Veal Dinner," said Marie.

"If they don't like it, we can play airplane with them," said Eddie. "That's what they did to us with the liver and wheat germ."

They went downstairs to feed Norton and Marigold, who were so hungry they would have eaten absolutely anything.

"I'm awfully thirsty," said Norton, shoveling more Veal Dinner into his mouth. "Could you please give me a little water to drink?"

"Sure, Dad," said Eddie with a sigh.

"I've been thinking," said Marigold in her funny little squeak. "Until we figure out how to get out of this mess your father got us into, we'll need to set things up down here so we can take care of ourselves."

"I had an idea about that," said Marie. "Remember that old dollhouse of mine, up in the attic? Maybe you could live in there for the time being."

"What a good idea," said Norton. "Kind of a little home within a home."

"I think we could make that work," said Marigold. "Why don't you go and get it, Marie?"

Eddie, who was starting to go up the cellar stairs, suddenly gasped. "Look! The window!"

He pointed to a small window high up on the basement wall that was at ground level outside the house. There, seeming to float behind the dirty glass, was a ghostly face.

"Mildred Grackle!" cried Marigold. "Quick! Hide! She's spying on us again! She can't see us like this!"

The tiny parents scooted behind the trash basket.

CHAPTER THREE

OOPS!

The four of them stood frozen in the basement for a minute. "Shoo! Shoo!" Marigold whispered, trying to make Mildred disappear.

"Be quiet, Marigold!" hissed Norton.

Eddie and Marie, getting their breath back, sprang into motion and bounded up the stairs, tripping over Basil again.

"That nosy witch!" said Eddie under his breath. "Every window in this house has her nose print on it!"

"Well, we really have to keep her away from here now," said Marie in alarm. "She can't see Mom and Dad!"

Mildred Grackle was not a witch, but she

looked like one. She had a big pointy nose, snaggle teeth, eyes like hot coals, and hair like barbed wire. All she needed was a big black hat. She lived with an extremely ugly and bad-tempered cat called Belladonna, and was always beating out rugs in front of her house, raising clouds of dirt that made people cough for blocks around. Her favorite activity was trying to snoop into other people's business.

Eddie and Marie flung open the front door. They could see Mildred at the side of the house, bent down in a very undignified position to peer into the basement window. She was wearing a pink quilted housecoat, and she had little curlers all over her head, rolled very tight.

"Um—can we help you?" said Marie loudly. Mildred stood up fast and patted her curlers, trying to collect herself.

"I need to see your parents, young lady," she said in a voice like a chain saw.

"They're not at home just now," said Marie, trying to be as polite as she could. "Can I tell them what it's about?"

"You can tell them what it's about, all right. It's about that stupid mutt of yours digging up my begonias and scaring my cat! That's what it's about." Basil growled at Mildred. She scowled at him, turned on her heel, and then marched across the cracked concrete driveway toward her house.

"Whew!" said Eddie. "That's over." Basil put his big cold nose into Eddie's hand. "I think you're going to have to stop digging up her garden, Basil," said Eddie. "She might turn you into an onion."

They went inside and closed the door.

Downstairs, Norton and Marigold were still hiding behind the trash can. "All clear," said Eddie. "You can come out now."

"Thank goodness," said Marigold. "I'm hungry."

"Oh, brother," said Eddie.

"Mom and Dad," said Marie, squatting on the floor beside them, "we're going to have to think about this thing. Eddie and I don't have the scientific knowledge to get you big again, and you're too little to do much for yourselves. I think we have to get some outside help. Let's call the police, okay?"

"No police! No police!" squeaked Norton.

For once, Marigold agreed with him. "We

can't have the police come snooping around here," she said firmly. "Why, once this invention is perfected, it'll make us millions! We'll get the Nobel Prize! I've got my speech prepared already. We can't have people with little minds stealing this invention away from us."

"Now hold on a second," interrupted Norton. "I'm the one who's giving the acceptance speech. It was my idea to begin with."

"It was not. It was mine," said Marigold.

"Mine! It was mine!"

"Would you two stop it? They're not going to give a Nobel Prize to a pair of two-inch people," said Marie in exasperation. "We have to get help from *someplace*."

"I know," said Eddie. "Why don't we call somebody from OOPS?"

"Hmmm," said Norton. "You might have an idea there."

OOPS, which stood for the Organization of Practical Scientists, was an association of peculiar people who were busy inventing toenail-cleaning machines, lettuce shredders, and other wonderful inventions in messy basements all over the country. There were probably about fifty members of

26

OOPS. This year Norton was serving his term as president.

"Hmmm," repeated Norton, rubbing his tiny chin.

"I don't know," said Marigold. "There are lots of people in OOPS who would sooner steal your idea than look at you."

"We'd have to find someone we trust absolutely," said Norton.

"Someone who doesn't need to steal ideas, because he has plenty of his own," Marigold added.

"Someone who's honest and pure."

"Someone who can keep a secret."

"Someone who can figure out how to get us out of this mess."

"Ozzie," they both concluded together.

Oswald Regenbogen, otherwise known as Ozzie, was head of the OOPS Crisis Task Force. He had gotten Norton and Marigold out of quite a few messes before. For instance, there was the time they had crossed a Venus's-flytrap with a dogwood tree to make a watchdogwood, a tree that would keep your front yard free of intruders. Unfortunately the trees got nasty, and Ozzie had to figure out how to get them under control. And then there was the time Norton and Marigold had invented instant-water powder, but couldn't figure out what to add to the powder to make the water. They had worked in the basement for six solid weeks until Ozzie had just told them to forget it. And, of course, there was the talking toaster that wouldn't shut up. But there had never, never been anything quite *this* bad.

Within the membership of OOPS, Ozzie was rumored to be the smartest human being in the world. It was whispered that he had invented Detroit. It was also said that he had invented the buttonhole, and that nobody in the world had known what to do with all those billions of buttons until Ozzie Regenbogen came along.

The only reason he had never gotten famous was that he didn't care about being famous. He only cared about thinking. He thought all day and all night. He thought in the bathtub and while playing the saxophone. He drew little doodles and diagrams and mathematical formulas on napkins. Hardly anybody understood what Ozzie was thinking, even after he explained it.

Actually, there was one other reason why

Ozzie had never gotten famous, and that was his shyness. He wasn't just a little shy, like people who sit in the corner at parties or who find themselves answering "Fine, thank you," just out of pure nervousness when somebody says "Good morning." Ozzie Regenbogen was so shy he hardly ever left his house. He had most of his groceries delivered. He did not ever announce his incredible discoveries to the newspapers. And when there was a meeting of OOPS, he used a special one-way television-and-telephone hookup he had invented, so that he could see everybody and talk to them without actually going there. Nobody in OOPS knew what Ozzie looked like.

"Do you think he can figure this thing out over the phone?" asked Marigold.

"I've heard of him solving worse things than this on the phone," Norton pointed out.

"Great," said Eddie. "Let's get going. Where's his phone number? I'll call him up. That is, unless you think you can dial the phone, ha-ha-ha." He laughed a mirthless laugh.

"Young man, that kind of humor is not going to be appreciated, so you may as well just stop it right now," squeaked Marigold.

"I'm sorry, Mom," said Eddie. He struggled to be serious. "But it is a little funny, you have to admit. Okay, where's Ozzie's number?"

"You don't call Ozzie Regenbogen. He calls you," said Norton.

"What do you mean, he calls you?" said Marie. "How does he know he's supposed to call here?"

"He has his ways," said Norton. "Nobody knows what they are. But Ozzie calls you, that's all I know."

"Great," said Marie. "Ozzie calls us. Just great."

CHAPTER FOUR

Little House in the Basement

The next morning, Saturday, Eddie and Marie met at the kitchen table. Marie had orange soda and chocolate chips for breakfast. Eddie poured himself a three-day-old cup of coffee. He was wearing a T-shirt that had four large holes in the front.

"I thought Mom made you throw that shirt out," said Marie.

"I was sort of saving it. I couldn't stand to throw it out," said Eddie. He took a sip of the coffee. "Yucch, this stuff tastes awful," he said. He poured it into the sink and got himself some cold cereal and milk.

"I had some really weird dreams last night,"

said Marie, munching her chocolate chips. "I was being chased by a teensy army with darning needles for swords."

"I had weird dreams too," said Eddie, rubbing his eyes. "It would probably be weird if we *didn't* have weird dreams, considering what's going on in our house."

"You want to go up in the attic with me and look for my old dollhouse?" asked Marie with a yawn.

"Sure," answered Eddie. "We probably have about five minutes before they start yelling for food."

The Bicker attic wasn't like any other attic in Brooklyn, or even in the world. Norton and Marigold didn't save things like dusty photo albums or old baby quilts. They saved old welding equipment, pieces of heavy machinery, and parts from cars and motorcycles, because they might come in handy for an invention someday.

But when she was eight, Marie had put her foot down and insisted that her dollhouse had to stay.

And there it was, in the corner. Even in the dim light, covered with dust, it shone with perfection. The dollhouse had been given to Marie by her aunt Beth, and it had been Beth's when she was a girl. It had two stories, shingles on the outside, and flowered carpeting on the stairs. There were lace curtains on the windows, and real electric lights. The windows went up and down, and the doors opened and shut with painted china doorknobs. The house was full of old-fashioned, overstuffed furniture, including a four-poster bed in the upstairs bedroom.

"This should make a nice little home for them," said Marie with satisfaction, as she blew the dust off the top. "The ceilings look just about the right height."

They wrestled it down from the attic without losing any of the furniture and carried it down to the basement.

"We were wondering where you were," said Marigold. "We're starving."

"I had a terrible night's sleep on the floor," complained Norton.

"Stop complaining, Norton," said Marigold.

"We brought you the dollhouse," said Eddie. "It should make things easier."

They all inspected it together. Norton and

Marigold stepped inside it, and it seemed as though it had been made for them. They found tiny, tiny metal dishes and silverware in the kitchen cabinets, and the little kitchen table and chairs were just the right size.

"Whoever decorated this place," Marigold said, squinting at the purple leaves on the linoleum, "I hate their taste."

Norton climbed up the stairs, which were a bit steep, to the second floor. "Look," he called down, "the beds are actually soft, and there are blankets and everything."

"You can't cook here, but if we bring you a jar of baby food in the morning, you can eat it all day," suggested Marie. "We can even put an ice cube in the icebox, to keep food from spoiling."

"Good idea," said Marigold, tearing her eyes away from the kitchen floor.

"And now for the crowning touch," said Marie. She found the old, frayed cord that hung from the back of the dollhouse. After some searching amid the tangle of wires and extension cords that covered the floor, she found a place to plug it in.

Instantly the house was filled with light.

Fancy chandeliers blazed in the hallways, lamps lit up in the bedrooms, and the overhead light in the kitchen glowed pleasantly.

"I told you we'd be glad someday if we saved this dollhouse," said Marie.

"It's nicer than our house," said Eddie.

"I guess when it's bedtime, one of us will have to come downstairs and unplug the lights," said Marie.

"And we can cover up the whole thing with a cloth, just like a birdcage," added Eddie.

"Don't be funny," warned Marigold.

"No, I think that's a good idea," said Norton. "Give us some privacy."

"What I want to know," said Marigold, "is where we're going to set up our lab. If we can get some work done, we may be able to figure out how to fix the machine."

"It's too tiny in there!" said Marie.

"You can do incredible things with transistors," said Marigold firmly. "I'll give you a shopping list on Monday."

"Speaking of shopping," Eddie said, sitting on the floor, "we're going to need a way to get money. I was thinking maybe we could get money out of the bank machine with your card."

"It's in my wallet," said Marigold. "Just don't spend it all on science fiction books and bubble gum."

"What's your secret number, so we can use the machine?"

"It's 3–14–1879. Einstein's birthday."

"We should have known," said Marie.

"Ahem," said Norton. "I think it's breakfast time."

"Okay, I'll bring you a jar of Liver Dinner," said Eddie, getting up. "Sorry it doesn't have any wheat germ in it."

Just as he reached the top of the stairs, the doorbell began ringing. Not ringing, exactly; screaming was more like it. Eddie had never heard their doorbell being rung so insanely.

Had somebody come to tell them the whole neighborhood was on fire, and that they'd all better get out right away? He flung open the door, his heart pounding.

There stood Mildred Grackle, wearing her housecoat and hair curlers. This time, though, her face was covered with stuff that looked like mud, her mouth was working without making any sound, and her eyes were bulging almost out of her head.

"What happened? What's wrong?" asked Eddie. She looked as though she had been in armed combat.

"What's wrong? What happened?" she spluttered, wiping some of the beauty-treatment goo off her face with the back of her hand. "I'll tell you what happened. I'll tell you what's wrong. That criminal dog of yours sneaked into my backyard this morning and let out all my lemmings, that's what happened. And you know what's *going* to happen? I'M GOING TO KILL HIM, THAT'S WHAT'S GOING TO HAPPEN! Where is he? I'm going to flush him down my toilet! I'm going to take him to the Grand Canyon and drop him off!"

Eddie was so relieved that the neighborhood wasn't burning down that he hardly heard Mildred as she kept on raving about what she was going to do to Basil. He knew she wasn't really going to do anything to Basil, anyhow.

But he gradually did become aware of another sound, the sound of the telephone ringing again and again. Suddenly it stopped.

"EDDIE!" yelled Marie. "IT'S OSWALD REGENBOGEN ON THE PHONE!"

Eddie shut the door in Mildred Grackle's face.

CHAPTER FIVE

Nine Weeks
to Live

It was very hard not to laugh at Ozzie Regenbogen's voice. He sounded like a person who was holding his nose. But as soon as Marie felt a giggle rising up in her, she squashed it immediately. Laughing at Ozzie Regenbogen's voice would have been like laughing at Albert Einstein's ears.

"Oh," he said after she had told him what the problem was. "Sounds like a twitch in the neutron field. That happens sometimes. Never seen it happen to a person, though. Interesting problem."

There was a long silence on the line.

"Er—can you help us?" asked Marie finally.

"Ah. Help you," he said, as if that thought hadn't crossed his mind. "Hmmm. Help you. Well, it's possible. Can't guarantee anything, though. Interesting problem."

Marie got the chilling feeling that the problem was much more interesting to him than Norton and Marigold were.

"I'll tell you what," he said to Marie finally. In her mind's eye, she could see a funny man holding his nose on the other end of the phone. "I'll give this a think. Maybe talk to some other members of the Crisis Task Force about it. Meantime, I'll need to speak to one of your parents. Want to know how they built their machine. Could you put one of them on the phone?"

"Sure," said Marie. "Hold on a minute, okay?"

She ran down the stairs. "Mom! Dad!" she yelled. "One of you has to come upstairs with me and talk to Ozzie Regenbogen!"

"I'll come!" squeaked Marigold. "Your father will get all the facts wrong."

"I'd better do it," said Norton. "Who knows what *she'll* tell him!"

Marie snatched one of them up in each

hand, trying not to squeeze them too hard around the middle. Then she sprinted up the stairs again.

When they reached the kitchen, Norton and Marigold looked around as if they were in a foreign country.

"This place is a mess," said Marigold.

"I know, Mom. We've been busy," said Marie with a sigh. Then she set her parents down on the counter near the phone receiver.

"Let me talk to him first," demanded Marigold. Marie moved her so she could stand next to the mouthpiece.

"Ozzie," said Marigold. "Thanks for calling. Now, here's the thing. Norton attached the epsilon confabulator onto the wrong end."

Ozzie's voice came buzzing out of the earpiece like a bee in a bottle.

"What?" yelled Marigold. "I can't hear you." She left the mouthpiece, ran over to the earpiece, and put her head against it.

Ozzie's voice buzzed a question and Marigold ran back to the mouthpiece to answer it. "Positive," she called.

Now Norton walked over to the phone and

stood near the earpiece. "I'll listen. You talk," he told his wife.

The phone buzzed again as Ozzie spoke.

"HE WANTS TO KNOW WHICH WAY THE VECTOR FIELD WAS POINTING," Norton yelled to Marigold.

"North," said Marigold smugly. "The right way."

Norton listened to yet another question from Ozzie, and his face fell.

"HE SAYS WE'RE BOTH WRONG!" he called to Marigold. "SAYS HE'LL HAVE TO THINK ABOUT IT. WE MAY HAVE SET UP A DOOLEY-BENZ WAVE PATTERN. HE'LL CALL US BACK TOMORROW, HE SAYS."

"Good-bye, Ozzie," squeaked Marigold into the mouthpiece. "We'll talk to you soon."

"He wants to talk to you again, Marie," Norton said. "Can we go downstairs and have a little snack now?"

Marie picked up the receiver, and Eddie picked up their parents. He headed downstairs with them.

"Hello?" said Marie nervously. She wasn't

42

sure why, but Ozzie Regenbogen made her uncomfortable. She wasn't sure he was quite human.

"What day did your parents get small?" he asked her.

"Yesterday," she answered. "Why?"

"Well, I've made some calculations. I figure they have about nine weeks to live. Give or take."

"WHAT?"

Eddie had come back upstairs, and was watching Marie closely.

"You know, of course," said Ozzie, "that very small animals have short life spans. They have such fast metabolisms, burning food up very quickly and whatnot, that they burn themselves out at quite a clip. Well, it's the same with your parents now."

"Could you be wrong about this?" said Marie, whose heart was suddenly beating as fast as any mouse's.

Ozzie seemed taken aback by the question. "Of course not," he said, sounding injured. "So we'll have to work this out fast. I'd say we have a two-in-seven chance of reversing the effects before it's too late. Good-bye."

He hung up abruptly, leaving Marie staring openmouthed at the phone.

"What was *that* about?" Eddie asked.

Marie hung the phone up slowly.

"They're going to die in nine weeks if we can't get them big again," she said. "Their lives have been speeded up, he says. Because they're so small."

"I thought they looked a tiny bit older just now," said Eddie.

"I don't want them to die," said Marie. A big tear rolled down her cheek. "I love them. Even if they're not normal parents."

"It's *better* that they're not normal parents," said Eddie. "And they're not going to die. We're not going to let them."

A tiny, squeaky voice wafted up from the basement. "Are there any more mashed bananas?" it called.

CHAPTER SIX

The Wrath of Mildred

A gray, sleet-filled week began, with no more word from Ozzie Regenbogen. Eddie and Marie trudged off to school and trudged home again. They had a hard time keeping their minds on their schoolwork.

Later that afternoon they stopped off at the radio hobby store and bought a whole collection of things that Norton and Marigold had requested for their lab: transistors, printed computer circuits, very fine wire, and several items Eddie and Marie could hardly see, let alone identify. Their parents immediately began setting up a lab in the family room of the dollhouse.

On Tuesday, Eddie's best friend Lewis

called to see if Eddie wanted to work on Lewis's model battleship with him, but Eddie's heart wasn't in it.

That night Marie was sitting in the living room munching on a dinner of Cheeze Dandies and watching the eleven o'clock news, when Eddie wandered in. He was eating a dish of rum raisin ice cream.

". . . And that's the bad news about the weather, everybody," the weatherman was saying. "Back to you, Bob."

"Well, folks," said Bob with a grin, "here's a really weird one from Long Island. It seems that a pack of lemmings has been seen heading up the Brooklyn–Queens Expressway. That's right, a pack of lemmings. And yesterday several people walking their dogs on Jones Beach saw this same pack of little brown rodents disappear into the Atlantic Ocean. Nobody knows how they got to New York, because their normal habitat is the Arctic Circle! Quite a little puzzle for the scientists, isn't it? And now, here's Trixie with the sports."

Eddie turned the television off. "Oh, cripes, those have to be Mildred's lemmings," he said. "I

46

forgot all about them. We're in big trouble now."

"Basil's in trouble, anyway," said Marie. "He's the one that let them out."

"Liberated them," Eddie corrected her. "At least they died with honor, their own way."

"Mildred's going to be wild when she hears about it," said Marie. "This is not what we need right now."

In fact, they hadn't seen Mildred Grackle in days, which was unusual and a little surprising, considering what had happened. She didn't even seem to be looking in the windows.

On Thursday afternoon the doorbell rang and Eddie answered it. A small man in a striped suit stood on the stoop. He had a skinny little mustache, like someone from an old movie.

"Hello there, young fellow," said the man.

Hello there, young fellow? Eddie stared at him.

"Are your parents about?" asked the man. He stood on tiptoe and peered around Eddie into the house.

Eddie moved a little to block his view. "They're busy right now. Can I give them a message?"

"Norton and Marigold Bicker, isn't that

right?" said the man, still trying to look over Eddie's shoulder.

"That's right," said Eddie. He was beginning to feel very edgy.

The man smoothed his mustache with his thumb and forefinger. "I have something for them," he said, with an unpleasant smile.

"You can give it to me," said Eddie.

"I'm supposed to give it to them."

"They're both really sick right now," said Eddie. "Incredibly sick." He felt as though a big "L" for Liar must be burning on his forehead.

"All right," said the man. "I've got to go. But you will promise to give it to them, won't you?" Eddie nodded, and the man pulled a grimy white envelope out of his jacket.

"Nice working with you, young fellow," he said with a wink. He turned and ran down the stairs. Eddie shut the door, mystified.

"What was that?" asked Marie, coming up from the basement with an empty jar of Peas and Carrots in her hand.

Eddie ripped open the envelope and studied the paper inside, trying to make sense of it.

"Looks official," he said.

Marie took the paper from him and moved toward the light so she could read the small print better. "Oh, great," she said. "Wonderful. It's a summons."

"A summons?"

"Yeah. Mildred Grackle is suing us. 'Loss of Lemmings,' it says here. Mom and Dad are supposed to appear in court next Wednesday."

Basil, sitting in the corner, scratched himself energetically behind the ear.

CHAPTER SEVEN

Shadow Dancing

Wednesday came and Wednesday went, but Norton and Marigold did not appear in court. They were completely preoccupied with setting up their tiny new lab. Besides, you can't appear in court if you're two and a half inches tall.

"Lots of people don't show up in court," said Marigold. "And we have a better excuse than most. We'll deal with it when we're big again."

If you're big again, thought Marie, studying her mother's tiny face. Were there a few more lines on it, or was it just her imagination? "Oh, where is that Ozzie Regenbogen, anyway?" she said. "And who says he's right about everything? I think he's weird."

"He'll call, he'll call," said Marigold. "Things have to kind of ferment in his mind. And he *is* right about everything. No one has ever heard of his being wrong."

Marie's heart sank a little further. Why didn't he call? Time was running out!

"Mildred shouldn't have been raising lemmings for fur coats anyway," said Eddie, coming down the basement stairs with an ice cube for the little plastic refrigerator. "It's cruel and unusual."

"Just like Mildred," said Marie.

"Especially the unusual part," snickered Eddie.

"Sssh!" warned Norton, darting behind the workbench. "The window!" Everybody froze.

Sure enough, a large shadow was darkening the basement window. Two shadows, in fact. Mildred had brought someone with her.

"Down there," she whispered, in a voice that could have been heard in Ohio. "I'm sure they're down there!"

"Why are you so sure?" asked a man's voice.

"They didn't appear in court, their car hasn't moved in a week, nobody has seen them—I'm absolutely positive those children murdered their parents. They're horrible little creatures. They always have been. If you search the basement, I know you'll find the bodies. I'm never wrong about things like this!"

"All right, pumpkin, I'll make sure it's looked into. Now can we go home and eat some goulash, please? I'm freezing."

The blood of the entire Bicker family ran as cold as ice when they recognized the deep, slow voice of Mildred's boyfriend, Lenny. Lenny was a sergeant with the New York City police force. He was not too bright, however.

The shadows moved away.

"Good grief," said Norton in disbelief. "She thinks you killed us."

"He calls her pumpkin," snorted Eddie. "Pumpkin."

"It would be funny, if I could remember how to laugh," said Marie. Then she laughed anyway.

"The thing is," said Eddie, "if the cops come, we won't be able to prove we *didn't* kill you. We can't very well bring you to the door in our hands."

"You know, it might not be so bad if we just

came right out with this thing," said Marie. "We need help, lots of help. And soon."

"We have all the time in the world," said Marigold testily. "And once we start asking people for help, the whole world is going to know about the Proton Enlarger. Revolutionary inventions get stolen from little people like us just like *that*." She snapped her microscopic fingers.

"No joke intended," said Marie under her breath.

"I'm not giving up my Nobel Prize so some fancy college scientist can grab it away from me," Marigold concluded. "No, indeed. We're waiting for Ozzie to call."

"What are we going to do in the meantime?" inquired Norton. "The police will be ringing the doorbell any minute."

"We have to convince Mildred that you're alive and well," said Eddie. "And I've got an idea."

"Such a bright boy," said Marigold, beaming. "He must get it from me."

By the time it was dark, Eddie had the whole thing set up. The window shades were all pulled down tight. Eddie had gone over to his friend Lewis's house and borrowed his high-intensity photographer's lamp, and it was set up next to the sofa. A Fred Astaire record was on the record player, ready to start. Marie had her jacket on. And Norton and Marigold were standing on the coffee table.

"Okay, are you ready?" whispered Eddie.

"Ready," squeaked Norton and Marigold.

"I guess so," said Marie.

"All right, here we go," said Eddie tensely.

"Hold it, hold it," whispered Marie. "I forgot my cup." She ran into the kitchen and returned in a second with a china cup. "Okay, now we can start," she said.

Eddie switched on the lamp and turned the record player on very loud. Norton and Marigold started dancing the fox trot. Marie slipped out the door.

In five minutes she was back again, giggling uncontrollably.

"What happened? Tell us everything!" demanded Marigold.

"Keep dancing! Keep dancing!" whispered Eddie urgently.

Norton and Marigold resumed dancing, while Marie caught her breath. "Well, I rang her bell," she began, wiping tears of suppressed laughter from her eyes, "and she came to the door. She was shocked to see me. And I said, very sweetly, 'Can I please borrow a cup of sugar, Ms. Grackle? My parents are so busy working these days, we're running out of everything!'" She started giggling again.

"And? And?" prompted Eddie.

"And when she came back with the sugar, I started talking very casually about the weather. Then I said, 'Oh, look at that, isn't it wonderful, my parents are finally taking a break, they're even dancing,' and I pointed over at our living room window. And there you were! The plan really, really worked! These big shadows were projected right onto the window shades, so it looked like you were your regular size, just dancing away!"

"What did Mildred do?" asked Eddie.

"She just about jumped out of her slippers," said Marie.

"Eddie, you're a genius," said Norton, trying to do a fancy twirl with Marigold. "Where did you get that idea, anyway?"

"It was on the Late Late Movie the other night," Eddie said modestly. "I thought it might work."

Marigold broke free of Norton. "You two should not be staying up so late," she said. "And when was the last time you had any vegetables? This place is a mess, too."

"I wouldn't have had this good idea if I hadn't watched the Late Late Movie," said Eddie. "And we just had some vegetables for breakfast, didn't we, Marie?"

"What kind of vegetables?" asked Marigold. Her eyes narrowed with suspicion.

"Potato chips. Potatoes are a vegetable."

"When we're big again, things won't be so whoopee," said Marigold. "You just wait and see, Mr. Big Shot."

"Um, I guess I better go put this cup of sugar away," said Marie, edging toward the kitchen.

CHAPTER EIGHT

Ozzie Has a Brainstorm

In the middle of the night the phone rang.

Eddie and Marie both snapped awake instantly, their hearts pounding. They spilled out of their rooms together and were in the kitchen by the third ring.

"Hello!" said Marie.

"Good evening." Marie recognized the nasal voice instantly. "Regenbogen here. I've figured it out. Just came to me, right in the middle of a dream. I was eating an ice-cream cone in King Tut's tomb, and there was the solution, written right on the wall of the pyramid."

"You know how to get them big again?" asked Marie.

59

"I know how they got themselves small. It's the Random Occipitor."

"What's the Random Ox-whatever?"

"Random Occipitor. It's a little gadget they must have used in their machine. Produces startling changes in molecule size, sometimes. Also makes the function of the machine a bit—well, unpredictable."

"What do you mean?" asked Marie.

"You can't build a machine that enlarges or reduces without a Random Occipitor," said Ozzie. "And that means you'll never be able to predict what your machine will do. Might make things smaller, might make things larger. You just don't know."

There goes the Nobel Prize, thought Marie.

"So, can we get them big again?" she asked. "Before it's too late?"

"It's possible," replied Ozzie. "We can try using the machine on them again. See what happens. There's a fifty percent chance they'll be restored to their former size. If you do it quickly, they won't be much the worse for wear."

Eddie was rubbing his eyes sleepily, trying to read the conversation in Marie's face.

"And what happens if the machine doesn't

work? What's the other fifty percent chance?" asked Marie.

"They'll be reduced so much that they'll be atomized."

Marie gulped. "Is trying this our only hope?" she asked at last.

"That's it," he said. "And I've figured out something else, too. Bit of a problem."

Marie could hardly bear to find out what it was.

"Your parents made an error when they calculated their polar alignment. For the machine to work properly, it has to be set up exactly twenty-three feet to the north of where it is now. Good-bye."

And he hung up.

"That man is unbearably weird," said Marie. "I just hope he's right." She repeated for Eddie everything Ozzie had said.

"Twenty-three feet to the north," said Eddie, frowning as he figured out the geography. "Let's see . . . that would be toward East Eighth Street, about the center of the next house . . ." His eyes opened very wide. "Holy cow! Do you know where that is?"

"No, where?"

"Right in the middle of Mildred Grackle's living room, that's where. How are we ever going to do that?"

"We'll figure it out," said Marie. "We have to. Besides, that's not the biggest worry we have. What if it doesn't work, and it atomizes them?"

"I guess we have to let them decide whether they want to take the risk."

"This is horrible," said Marie. "I don't want to be an orphan. I wish they had never built the stupid thing."

"So do I," agreed Eddie. "So do I."

❄❄ CHAPTER NINE ❄❄

Life or Death

At six o'clock the next morning it was so bitterly cold and windy that the frost-covered windows rattled in their frames. Eddie and Marie were downstairs in the basement, dressed in several layers of clothing. Their parents were sitting together in an old mitten of Marie's, which was pulled all the way up to their chins. They were eating applesauce from a thimble.

Basil, who had been allowed into the basement for the first time, sniffed curiously at Norton and Marigold. Eddie and Marie kept a close eye on him, making sure he didn't try anything funny.

Marie's teeth were chattering, and she wasn't

sure it was just from the cold. The moment of decision had arrived. There had been very little sleep for her or Eddie that night, and they had finally decided that they might as well just go downstairs at sunrise and get it over with.

Eddie was explaining the situation to Norton and Marigold for the second time.

"If there's a fifty-fifty chance that we could be atomized," Marigold mused, "maybe we shouldn't do it. Maybe we should just live the rest of our lives tiny. We could get used to it in a couple of years, I guess."

"You can't do that," said Eddie grimly.

"Why not, for heaven's sake?" asked Marigold. "People get used to all sorts of things. I got used to being married to your father."

Norton harrumphed. "*Some* people have had even *worse* people to get used to," he said.

Eddie and Marie were exchanging looks with each other, trying to decide whether to tell their parents the awful truth. Finally Eddie shrugged and Marie nodded.

"It's not as simple as that," said Marie. "You can't *have* a couple of years to get used to it."

"Why not?" said Norton.

Marie swallowed hard. "Because Ozzie Regenbogen says you only have about eight weeks to live. Your lives are speeded up, like little tiny animals'."

"Maybe Ozzie's wrong," said Marigold. She looked panic-stricken. "Maybe he didn't figure it out right."

"Ozzie's never wrong. We both know that Ozzie's never wrong," said Norton.

"Eight weeks! Why, that's no time at all! Norton, we're going to die in eight weeks!" Marigold threw her tiny arms around his tiny shoulders, weeping little tiny tears.

"Good-bye, my darling!" cried Norton. "Farewell, my love!" He blew his nose on a little corner of the mitten.

"Norton, you know I never meant all those awful things I said to you, don't you?"

"I know, sugarplum. I never meant all those terrible things I said to you, either."

"I don't know where I'd be without you!" Marigold dissolved into tears again.

"Be brave, my darling!" said Norton. "We'll die together, hand in hand."

They finished the applesauce together.

Eddie looked at the floor and cleared his throat. "Mom? Dad?" he said. "What if we tried the machine again?"

"The machine! Yes! Of course!" cried Norton and Marigold together. It was clear that they had forgotten about it.

"Okay," said Marie decisively. "We'll get everything ready. You just wait here." She turned on her heel and marched up the stairs. Eddie followed her.

"Whew!" she said, leaning against the upstairs door. "That was really heavy."

"Yeah, I think I like it better when they scream at each other."

"Okay," said Marie. "We're ready for Phase One. This better work. This just better work. I don't know what I'll do if they end up—"

"Don't think about it. It'll work, that's all."

"Okay," said Marie. "I'll start looking for that key. I know we have it someplace."

Eddie hitched up his shoulders, stood up very straight, and marched across the kitchen toward the phone. On his way he grabbed a blue dish towel.

He picked up the phone and dialed Mildred

Grackle's number. Then he quickly crumpled up the dish towel and held it to the mouthpiece.

"Grackle?" he said in his deepest, gruffest voice when she answered the phone. "Mildred Grackle?"

Oh, please, he thought, don't let me sound like Eddie Bicker talking through a dish towel.

"You think the Bicker kids knocked off their parents, right?" he snarled. "Well, I have some information that just might interest you. Meet me at the skating rink in Rockefeller Center at two o'clock this afternoon."

"Who is this? Who is this?" she shrilled.

"Never mind who this is," said Eddie. "Just be there."

"How will I find you?"

Suddenly the light of pure deviltry shone in Eddie's eyes. "You won't find me, I'll find you. Carry a chicken in your left hand. Not the right one, the left."

He hung up the phone.

"There," he said, amazed that he'd gotten away with it. "That should buy us a good couple of hours. She'll have to go all the way into the city, wait around, give up, and come all the way back. And there aren't a lot of trains running at that time of day."

"Okay," said Marie. "But we still have to hurry."

While she spoke, she was rummaging frantically through the old corks, plastic bags, apple corers, and birthday candles that filled the junk drawer. "Aha! Here it is!" she yelled, holding up an old key on a frayed piece of string. "I knew it was in there someplace!"

"Are you sure it's the key to Mildred's house?"

"Yes, it's the one she lent us the day her lemming cages were delivered. She never came and got it back. Perfect!"

"Okay, now I have to call Lewis," said Eddie, dialing the phone again.

"Hold on, Eddie," said Marie. "Are you sure we ought to bring Lewis into this?"

"He's my best friend, Marie."

"I know, but can we trust him absolutely? And what if there's danger? Do you want to risk exposing him to it?"

"He was here for the watchdogwood experiment. Remember, one of them almost got him? He never even told his parents."

"All right," said Marie reluctantly. "I don't think we can do this without him, anyhow. I just hope he's not totally weirded out."

Eddie finished dialing the phone.

"Lewis, it's Eddie. I need your help on an important project. . . . What? . . . I know it's six thirty. Just listen to me for a second, will you? Can you come over this afternoon? About a quarter to two. It's life or death. But you can't ask any questions, okay? . . . No, this isn't another one of my stupid jokes. This is REAL LIFE! Okay, thanks. Don't be late." He hung up.

"I sure hope he's still good at keeping his mouth shut," said Eddie. "Because he's going to have a lot to talk about."

They spent the rest of the morning making preparations and getting instructions from Norton and Marigold. They dragged some spare boards from the workshop and used them to build a ramp up the basement stairs. Eddie noticed that his hands were clammy from nervousness. At lunchtime Marie dropped two glasses and a bowl full of Frosty Crunch. Even Basil was nervous, walking around the house in endless little circles and not lying down at all.

At about one, Eddie and Marie stationed

themselves behind the curtains in the living room, watching Mildred Grackle's house. In Mildred's bedroom window they could see the end of the powerful telescope she had just installed. It was pointed straight at their house.

There was no sound but the ticking of the clock. If Mildred didn't leave her house, their plan would fall apart.

"There she goes!" whispered Eddie at a quarter after one. "Wait, there's something yellow hanging out of her pocketbook. It's chicken feet!" He couldn't restrain a whoop of glee.

"Okay, call Lewis and tell him to come over *now*," said Marie. She was in no mood for fooling around.

Eddie sprinted for the phone. "I know it's early," Marie heard him say. "Will you just *come*?"

In three minutes the doorbell rang. There stood Lewis, tall and red-haired, looking very perplexed.

"Downstairs," said Marie. She started to lead him to the basement door. She was glad Lewis was a big kid.

"Just a second." Eddie threw out an arm to

stop Lewis. "Before you go down there, I want you to swear something."

"What are you talking about?" said Lewis.

"You must swear on everything that is holy to you that you will never ever divulge what you see in this house today, even if it is stranger than anything you have ever seen in your life," said Eddie.

"Give me a break," snorted Lewis. "What is this, *The Exorcist*?"

"This is serious, Lewis. Now, I want you to swear."

"Okay, I swear."

"Pinky swear," added Eddie.

"Okay, pinky swear."

They walked down to the basement. Norton and Marigold were just scampering behind the wastebasket, but it was too late. Lewis had already caught sight of them. He stopped dead in his tracks halfway down the ramp.

"Eddie, was that—?" he said in confusion.

"Lewis, say hello to my parents," said Eddie. Norton and Marigold came back out into the open.

"Um, hello, Mrs. Bicker. Um, hello, Mr.

71

Bicker." Lewis was the color of newly fallen snow.

"Hello, dear," said Marigold. "Nice to see you."

"Over here," said Marie, pointing to the contraption in the corner. "We have to move this machine up the stairs."

"You have got to be kidding," said Lewis, recovering himself a little. "That thing must weigh a zillion pounds."

"Lewis, this is life or death," said Eddie.

Very slowly and carefully, they managed to maneuver the machine onto a wooden dolly, and then wheel the dolly over to the stairway. Then, inch by inch, they began pushing it up the stairs.

Halfway up, Marie suddenly gasped. "I'm losing it! I can't hold it anymore!" The machine slid back to the bottom before they were able to stop it.

Marie had tears in her eyes. "I'm sorry," she said.

"It's okay," said Eddie. "We'll just start again."

They started again, going faster this time. With a last tremendous heave, they got it to the top of the stairs and into the kitchen.

"That was the hard part," panted Eddie. Their chests were all heaving. "Now we're home free."

In another fifteen minutes they had the thing wheeled right up to Mildred's front door. By now, Eddie was praying out loud. "Oh, please, oh, please let her not come home. Oh, please make her stay out until we're all done. I'll be good forever. I'll never eat another candy bar, and I'll never stay up for the Late Late Movie again."

Marie was fumbling with the lock. "It's not working," she said. "It's the wrong— Oh, here it goes." The door swung open.

Mildred Grackle's living room was filled with little china figurines of shepherd boys and pussycats and clowns. Some of them got broken as they wheeled the machine into place. "We'll have to replace those," said Marie.

Eddie looked at his watch. A quarter to three.

He grabbed Marie's hand, and they ran out the door. "Be back in a minute," he called to Lewis. "Hold the fort." Lewis looked terrified.

Eddie and Marie flew down the basement stairs. Norton and Marigold were standing together, looking inconceivably tiny. They were very calm.

On the workbench was a small package wrapped in brown paper. It had arrived as if by magic at the front door, very early that morning. Inside the package was what looked like an ordinary remote-control unit for a television, and a set of instructions written in a small, neat hand. The instructions were signed, "O. Regenbogen."

"I sure hope this thing works," said Eddie.

"It will work, dear," said Marigold. "Ozzie has just done a little rewiring on it, that's all."

"Okay," said Marie. "Let's go."

She bent down and picked Marigold up. Eddie picked Norton up, and they carried the two of them upstairs and over to Mildred's house. They put their parents down gently on the floor in front of the machine.

At last, everything was set to go. The machine was plugged in and humming.

"Epsilon confabulator," said Marie.

"Check," said Eddie.

"On switch," said Marie.

"Right-side up," said Eddie.

"Vector field," said Marie.

"Check," said Eddie.

"Polar multiplexer," said Marie.

"Ready to activate," said Eddie. "Everything's set just the way Ozzie told us to do it." He checked all the knobs and dials one last time.

Marie squatted down in front of her parents. "This will all be over in a second," she whispered.

"I know, dear, I know," said Marigold. "Now, go ahead on home."

"Don't worry," said Norton to Eddie and Marie. "You'll do just fine."

"Don't eat so much junk food," said Marigold. "And remember to brush your teeth."

Marie was starting to cry. "We'll see you in a couple of minutes," she said, and then she turned and walked out the door.

" 'Bye, Mom. 'Bye, Dad," said Eddie in a trembling voice. "C'mon, Lewis, let's go." Then he followed Marie.

On the front stoop of their own house, Eddie turned to Lewis. "Lewis," he said, "you've been a good friend. I think you should go home now. If anything awful happens, you shouldn't be here. I don't want you to have it on your conscience."

"Are you sure you don't need me?" said Lewis.

Eddie nodded, and Lewis shook his hand

gravely. Then he walked away, looking relieved. "Good luck," he called back.

In the basement, Marie already had the remote-control device in her hand. She was reading the instructions one more time.

"Ready?" said Eddie.

"Ready as I'll ever be," she replied.

"Okay, push Channel 2 and Channel 8 at the same time."

Marie pointed the end of the device at Mildred's house, shut her eyes tight, and pressed the buttons.

Incredibly, the black plastic began glowing a bright cherry red. "Ow!" said Marie, dropping the unit. "That's hot!"

There was a loud bang from the house next door, followed by a blinding flash of light. It was so bright that Eddie and Marie could see it through the small, dirty basement window. They gasped.

Then there was silence.

"It didn't work," said Marie.

"We never should have tried it," said Eddie.

Suddenly, Marie put her hand up, signaling Eddie to be quiet. "Shh," she said. "Listen." A familiar, and very loud, voice was wafting over to them on the breeze from Mildred's house.

"It was your fault to begin with!" yelled the voice. "We never should have used the Random Occipitor!"

"Oh, yeah, Mrs. Brilliant Inventor? What about that little problem with the vector field?" came the equally loud reply.

"Mom!" said Eddie.

"Dad!" said Marie. "They have big voices!"

"They're okay!" they whooped.

They dashed out of the house and burst into Mildred's living room. There, with her hands on her hips, was their mother. And beside her, with his fingers in his ears, was their father. And behind *them* was a very bizarre-looking stranger.

"Wh-who's that?" stammered Marie.

They all spun around to look. Staring emptily but pleasantly at Marigold was a six-foot-tall china milkmaid.

"Oops," said Marigold.

"I guess the Proton Enlarger ray was pointing at her too," said Norton.

"I think we'd better get her out of here before

Mildred gets home," said Eddie. "And the machine, too."

About half an hour later, Eddie looked out the window and saw Mildred Grackle coming home, carrying a bedraggled chicken by the feet.

Epilogue

Two weeks later, life had returned to normal in the Bicker household—as normal as things got in the Bicker household, anyway.

Mildred Grackle had been disappointed at first to see that Norton and Marigold were well and truly alive. But then she was cheered up by the fact that she could resume her lawsuit about the lemmings. A new court date was set. Several letters from Mildred about the matter were arriving in the mail every day.

And she didn't let up on the snooping, either. There seemed to be fresh Mildred-size nose prints on each window. She even sent Lenny on occasional walks past the Bickers' house to see what he could see.

Basil was under strict orders from Eddie and Marie to stay away from Mildred's backyard, her begonias, and her cat.

Norton and Marigold were not concerned about all this, however. They were working on a new invention, something about gravity.

Eddie and Marie were having regular bedtimes again.

"I have to admit it," said Marie to her brother in the hallway between their rooms one night. "I feel a lot better getting enough sleep. And eating some protein."

"I feel a lot better having regular-size parents," said Eddie, yawning and stretching. "Right here in their own bedroom."

All of a sudden there was a huge crash from the basement.

"I thought they were up here," said Eddie angrily, as they ran to the staircase.

"I'll never forgive them if they're fooling around with that machine again. This time they can just stay small," said Marie. "And I'll go find some normal parents."

At the top of the stairs, they bumped into Norton and Marigold.

"We thought you were—" said Eddie.

"Then who's downstairs?" said Marie.

They all charged down to see.

Standing in the middle of the basement was Mildred Grackle. She looked very sheepish. She was eight inches tall.

"Help," she peeped.

"Mildred, explain yourself!" demanded Norton.

"I just had to find out what you were always doing down here," she said. "So I came in the window." Sure enough, the basement window was wide open. She must have had quite a time climbing through it. "And then I saw that machine," continued Mildred, "and I thought I'd just press a few buttons to see what it did, and here I am. And . . . I'm so *hungry*." She broke down in tears, and her little curlers shook.

"Oh, Mildred, what are we going to do with you?" said Marigold.

Mildred stopped crying. "Well, can't you make me big again?" She stared at them. "You *have* to make me big again! If you don't make me big, I'll sue you for everything you've got! It was your machine that did this to me!"

A big smile spread across Eddie's face. "Speaking of suing," he said, "are you still going to sue us because our dog let out your lemmings? I was thinking that you might want to drop that lawsuit."

"I certainly will not!" she said. "I mean—er—um . . ." She fell silent as she began to grasp the difficulty of her situation.

"Perhaps you'd like to think about that a little more," said Eddie. "Especially since I've been doing some research. You're not allowed to have wild animals in your backyard in Brooklyn, New York, you know. Those were illegal lemmings."

"Oh. Oh, dear. Well, all right. . . . But, I mean . . . what about me? Look what's happened to me. Aren't you going to get me out of this mess?"

"We'll think about it," said Marigold slowly.

And they all thought about it for a very long time.